Cherry and Olive

Cherry and Olive

Benjamin Lacombe

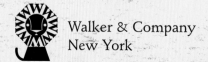
Walker & Company
New York

Cherry Sullivan lives in an apartment
with her father. She often looks out
the window to watch other children
playing and wishes for a friend. And
every morning she sees her father's
gray truck parked in front of the animal
shelter where he works.

Cherry likes almost everything, especially chocolate and cheese. What does she dislike? Cherries. In cakes and candy and especially in the jam that her mother loved so much.

Cherry also devours books: comic books about pirates, Jules Verne novels, and a guide to birds. The guide even teaches her how to talk to birds. Cooing, twittering, clucking, and quacking—she knows all kinds of bird calls.

At school, Cherry stays quiet so no
one will notice her.

"Cherry Sullivan, come up to the
blackboard!" the teacher calls. "If we need
twelve strawberries to prepare a jar of
jam, how many do we need to prepare
five jars?"

Cherry hears kids snickering behind
her: "With that Cherry, we could make
tons of jam!"

During recess, Cherry sits alone on a bench at the end of the playground with a book in her lap.

"Books are definitely more interesting than those kids!" she thinks. Then she gets lost in her book and imagines having a wonderful adventure flying around the world in a hot-air balloon.

But there's one boy who seems like a hero from one of Cherry's books—the handsome Angelo. He always has a group of girls flocking around him on the playground. Cherry would never dare to join in.

Sometimes Cherry sees him at the library. But she hides behind the bookshelves so that he doesn't see her.

Since her mother left, Cherry has helped her father after school at the animal shelter, cleaning the animals' cages. One day, she notices that the last cage is strangely quiet. Cherry walks over and finds an adorable, wrinkly little dog.

"Hello, sweet puppy!" she says.

The dog lifts its head and wags its tail. It's happy to see her!

"I'm going to call you Olive, my round little friend," she says proudly.

Cherry and Olive become the best of friends and do everything together. They go for walks, play fetch, and even cuddle up for naps.

Her father warns her not to become too attached. "Olive doesn't belong to you. At any moment her owner might come to the shelter and take her home."

Cherry begins to cry. "No, Dad. Please don't let them take away my only friend!"

"I'm sorry, honey. If nobody comes to pick up Olive within one month, you may keep her. But if her owner comes before then, promise me you won't make a fuss about letting her go."

Cherry agrees, secretly hoping Olive's owner will never find her.

Whenever someone comes to the shelter,
Cherry takes Olive for a walk so no one will
see her. They wander under the weeping
willows, around the whale fountain, and past
the ice-cream man—but the walk is always
over too soon.

On the way to the park, the people they pass always point and stare at the odd-looking dog. Cherry knows just how sad Olive feels. She sticks her tongue out at them to stand up for her friend.

One day, as they are walking along, they run into Leah and Matilda, the two meanest girls at school.

"Look at Cherry and her stinky, wrinkly dog!" they shout. "It looks like it needs to be ironed."

Cherry, to her surprise, tells the girls to leave the dog alone. She has never dared to stand up to them before, and it feels very good.

On the day that Cherry has had Olive for exactly one month, they take their usual walk in the park. Cherry tells herself, "If we arrive at the whale fountain before the mail carrier arrives, Olive will stay with me." Unfortunately, the mail carrier is already there when Cherry and Olive reach the fountain.

Cherry doesn't give up hope. "If we arrive at the end of the park before the ice-cream man, Olive will stay with me." Unfortunately, the ice-cream man is already at the park exit.

Cherry wanders farther and farther, trying to make the walk last as long as possible before they have to return.

As they round the corner to the shelter, Cherry's heart sinks as she sees three people standing with her father. They must be Olive's owners. She wants to turn around and pretend she never saw them, but Olive pulls the leash out of her hands and runs and runs and runs, leaving Cherry standing alone.

Olive is excited to see her owners and jumps up and down. Cherry recognizes the boy with his parents. It's Angelo! He hugs his dog and turns toward Cherry.

"Thank you for taking care of her. We live just around the corner. Would you like to come and visit her sometime?" he asks.

"Oh yes!" Cherry answers, relieved and surprised.

Cherry and Angelo sit together, petting the dog. She even gets up enough courage to talk to him.

"By the way, what is your dog's name?" she asks.

"You don't know? Her name is Chocolate!" he replies.

Cherry smiles because chocolate is one of her favorite things of all, and so is having new friends.

Text and illustrations: Benjamin Lacombe
Copyright © 2006 Éditions du Seuil
Translation copyright © 2007 by Seuil Jeunesse
First published by Seuil Jeunesse in France in 2006 as *Cerise Griotte*

Published in the United States of America in 2007 by
Walker Publishing Company, Inc.
Distributed to the trade by Holtzbrinck Publishers

For information about permission to reproduce selections from
this book, write to Permissions, Walker & Company,
104 Fifth Avenue, New York, New York 10011

Library of Congress Cataloging-in-Publication Data
Lacombe, Benjamin.
[Cerise Griotte. English.]
Cherry and Olive / Benjamin Lacombe.
p.   cm.
Summary: A very shy girl who longs for a friend falls in love with a lost puppy
at the shelter where her father works.
ISBN-13: 978-0-8027-9707-0 • ISBN-10: 0-8027-9707-5 (hardcover)
[1. Bashfulness—Fiction. 2. Dogs—Fiction. 3. Animals—Infancy—Fiction.
4. Animal shelters—Fiction. 5. Teasing—Fiction. 6. Friendship—Fiction.] I. Title.
PZ7.L13567Che 2007   [E]—dc22   2007006671

Visit Walker & Company's Web site at www.walkeryoungreaders.com

Printed in Belgium

2 4 6 8 10 9 7 5 3 1

To my mother,
To Lili and Seb,
For Mia, Justine, Balint, and Loris,
A hug to Gigi who became Olive
when I wrote this story,
A big thanks to Rebecca, Justine Brax,
and Françoise Mateu for their
invaluable advice.